TERRY DEARY

THE Vampire OF CROGLIN

With illustrations by
Stefano Tambellini

Barrington Stoke

First published in 2008 in Great Britain by
Barrington Stoke Ltd
18 Walker Street, Edinburgh, EH3 7LP

www.barringtonstoke.co.uk

This edition first published 2015

A CIP catalogue record for this book is available from the British Library upon request

ISBN: 978-1-78112-458-1

Printed in China by Leo

Contents

Chapter 1
The Stranger

Let me tell you about Croglin. Let me tell you about the horrors that happened at the Hall back in 1780. Autumn 1780 till summer 1781. Eight months of mystery, when I was a boy. My name is Tom Taylor and Croglin is where I live.

Croglin is a village so sleepy that even the dogs don't bark. Not even at strangers.

The cats sleep in the summer sun, bees buzz and sheep munch. Birds sing in the trees and in the skies. But they never sing in the churchyard. That's odd, isn't it?

"That's odd," a cart driver said to me.

"What's odd?"

"The silence in the churchyard," the cart driver said.

"Well, the dead don't make a lot of noise," I said with a shrug.

"No ... but all those trees. Why aren't there birds singing?" he asked. It was a warm day. He mopped his brow with a dirty scarf. "It's as quiet as a grave," he said.

"Is that meant to be a joke?" I asked. The grey gravestones leaned like drunken men in the long grass. When the winter winds came they shook the earth and made the gravestones as loose as Parson Perkins' rotten teeth. It wasn't always summer in Croglin.

Croglin is just a cluster of twenty cottages. Small, low, stone cottages with straw roofs to keep out the storms.

Twenty cottages, the church, the tavern, Parson Perkins' house ... and Croglin Hall.

"Croglin Hall, I'm headed for," the cart driver said. "Where is that then?"

I pointed to the low house that stood behind the low graveyard wall. The carter shivered. "Nice view from there! Who wants to look at a graveyard?"

"I do," said a harsh man's voice.

We swung round and saw the man standing in the middle of the path. The road was so dusty we hadn't heard his horse. He was young and his face was wind-burned brown. He jumped to the ground and walked towards us. "Leave our furniture at Croglin Hall and stop asking questions," he snapped.

The carter jumped onto his cart and cracked his whip. The cart rumbled and creaked away. There was a cry as it turned the corner too fast. It had almost knocked over Parson Perkins.

The parson trotted and sweated along the road towards the man. I sat on our garden wall and watched. The parson twisted his hands and bowed his head. "You must be the new tenant of Croglin Hall."

"I am Michael Ransome," the man said. "We have rented the Hall for seven years."

"We?" The parson grinned and showed the rotten stumps of teeth.

"I'll be living here with my brother Edward, and my sister Amelia," the man

said. “We’ve come from Australia so Amelia can have the peace and rest she needs.” The young man began to lead his horse down the road.

“When will your sister be ...?” Parson Perkins began.

“They are following in a carriage. Amelia is not strong. We could not expect her to ride. They will be here tomorrow,” Michael Ransome said and strode off in clouds of dust.

“You are welcome in the church every Sunday,” the parson called after him.

“We’ll be there,” the man replied without looking back.

“I hope you will be happy and safe in Croglin Hall,” Parson Perkins cried.

The young man stopped suddenly. “Safe? What do you mean?” he barked.

"Oh ... nothing," the parson whined and twisted his bony hands till they were red as a sunset.

The parson gave me a warning look with his watery grey eyes. The look said, "Say nothing."

I said nothing.

Chapter 2
The Angel

The next day the children gathered in the road. We had rushed to finish our jobs – feeding the hens, driving the sheep onto the common, gathering firewood and berries from the hedges.

The clusters of berries were thick in the churchyard brambles. “Go and pick them, Tom,” Alice Marley dared me.

“No,” I said.

"Scared?" she mocked.

"No."

"Go and pick them then."

"No-o!" I shouted.

Alice Marley had dirty yellow hair and a runny nose, a missing tooth where her father had punched her, and she smelled of the cows she slept with. I think I was in love with her. But I wouldn't pick the churchyard berries. Not even for Alice Marley.

"You're scared." Alice sniffed and wiped her nose on her sleeve.

"The Croglin Vampire sucks blood and he stores the blood in the berries," I told her. "Everybody knows that. I am not eating berries full of blood."

Alice smiled her gap-tooth smile. “I would.”

I looked at her hard. “You wouldn’t.”

“I would.”

“I’d like to see that,” I spat.

She reached over the low stone wall. She grasped a fat berry between her finger and thumb. She pulled it away from the bramble bush. The rest of the village children watched and held their breath. Alice put the berry in her mouth.

She closed her jaws and crushed the berry. She smiled.

Then the smile slid from her face. A trickle of red juice ran from the corner of her mouth. She grabbed at her throat and gasped. She sank to the ground and rolled in the grass by the wall. Her tongue was purple-red.

"Ahhhh!" she said, choking.

"What is it, Alice?" Elsie Brown cried.

"Blood!" Alice gasped.

We all jumped away from her in horror.

"Blood?" I whispered. "What can we do, Alice?" I didn't want to see my true love die that way.

"You ... can ..." she panted.

"Yes, Alice?"

She sat up with a sudden-sweet smile. "You ... can ... get me some more of them. They're lovely!" She giggled.

"Lovely? Blood tastes lovely?" Elsie cried.

Alice jumped to her feet and dusted grass off her grey skirts. She stood nose-to-nose with Elsie Brown. "They're berries. Plain berries. They're not full of blood and there is no Croglin Vampire."

I started to argue. "My mother says ..."

"Your mother is a fool. The same as you." She laughed and poked me in the chest with a dirty finger. "Have you ever seen the Vampire?"

"No, but I have seen something you've never seen," I said angrily and pushed her bony finger away.

"Oh, yes? What have you seen, terrified Tommy?"

"I've seen the grandest coach ever to drive through Croglin village!"

"Liar!" she snorted.

"He's not lying," Elsie told her. "Look behind you, Alice."

Alice swung round. A fine black coach, pulled by four white horses, had stopped at the gates of Croglin Hall. "It's the strangers, come to live at the Hall!" Elsie cried.

We had rushed through our work that morning because we wanted to see this moment and we'd almost missed it. A young man stepped from the coach. He was handsome and as berry-brown as his brother. "That must be Edward Ransome ... handsome Ransome," Alice said with a giggle.

The stranger opened the Croglin Hall gates to let the coach drive through. He closed the gates behind it. We raced over to peer through the bars.

The carriage stood at the front door of the house and the older brother, Michael, came out to open the carriage door. He held out a hand and helped a young woman down.

Her dress was the finest sea-green silk and her bonnet was as large as a porridge pot. Under it, I could see her face was sickly pale. She stopped and looked towards the gate. She smiled at us.

Parson Perkins had told us about people like her.

"She's an angel," I whispered.

"Tah!" Alice Marley spat. "She's as ugly as our goat ... and I hate her!"

Chapter 3
The Visitor

Autumn turned to winter. Every Sunday the church was full.

The villagers had not come to praise God. The villagers had not come to hear Parson Perkins preach.

The villagers had come to look at Miss Amelia Ransome. She drifted down the church to the special seats at the front – the Croglin Hall seats. Michael sat on one side of her and Edward on the other.

Every week Amelia wore a new dress of finest silk. Men like my dad looked at her and their eyes shone like the candlelight on the dress.

"A lovely lass," he said one evening after church.

"She is a stuck-up snob and I hate her," my mother snarled and slopped cabbage onto his plate so it splashed his shirt.

"Alice Marley says that," I told them.

My dad shook his head. "Women, son," he whispered. "Just jealous."

Mother swung round and waved the meat knife under his nose. "She won't be so lovely when the Croglin Vampire sinks his teeth into her skinny, pasty neck!" she warned.

Dad shrugged. "We don't know for sure there's a vampire," he sighed.

Mother's lips were set in a grim smirk. "Remember what happened to the last young lady at Croglin Hall," she said. "Mark my words, Will Taylor, there is something evil out there and it will seek her out. Maybe tonight. It's a full moon tonight!"

"Shut up, woman, and serve my dinner," Dad muttered, but he didn't sound too happy.

Outside in the darkness an owl screeched. I shivered. That night I couldn't sleep. I heard footsteps running along the village road outside my window. Men and women called out in fear and anger. The church clock struck two.

It had struck three before the village fell silent again. Then there was only the sighing of the wind in the bare churchyard trees.

Next morning was cold and I wrapped cloths around my feet to keep them warm in the muddy lane that led to the sheep pens.

Alice Marley was waiting for me and there was joy in her eyes. "I see your vampire struck last night," she said.

"Did he?"

"Haven't you heard the news? Didn't your parents tell you?"

"They were asleep when I left the house," I said.

"They would be. It was a sleepless night," she said with a nod.

"But what happened?"

Alice sat on the wall and licked her lips. "The lovely Amelia Ransome went to bed at ten o'clock last night. She went into her bedroom and started to undress. But she didn't close the shutters ..."

"Why not?" Elsie Brown asked.

"Because no one could see into her bedroom. Her room faces the churchyard, doesn't it?"

"Does it?" I asked.

"All the men in the village know that," Alice said darkly. "Anyway, she was standing by her bed when she looked out of the window and saw two lights coming towards her from the churchyard. Through the trees and over her lawn."

"What did she do?" Elsie squeaked.

"She froze. Stood by her bed like an icicle."

"I'd have run for the door," I said.

"Ah, but the door is nearer the window than the bed. If she went towards the door she'd be going towards the eyes!"

"What eyes?" I asked.

"The two red lights! They were monster's eyes!" Alice said.

"Were they?"

"So they say. But the eyes vanished – maybe they went behind a bush. She made a dash for the door, but her hands were shaking too much to turn the key and unlock it."

"Why didn't she scream?" Elsie asked.

"Her throat was frozen. Then she heard a scratch, scratch, scratch at the window. She saw an evil brown face with glowing eyes looking in at her. She ran back to the bed. The scratching stopped."

"That's good," I said.

"That was bad," Alice Marley cried. "A bony finger was starting to peck at the glass in the window. Peck! Peck! Crack!"

"Crack?"

"It broke the glass ... a bony white hand reached through the hole and opened the latch on the window!" Alice paused. She jumped down from the wall and stretched.

"And then?" Elsie and I cried.

"And then ... I'll tell you later ... I have sheep to see to," Alice said and walked up the lane.

Chapter 4
The Shadow

Alice skipped down the lane towards the moors and Elsie Brown and I raced after her. "You can't stop there!" I panted.

"Can't I?" Alice asked. "Why can't I?"

"You have to tell us what happened next!" Elsie wailed.

"No I don't," Alice said.

"I'll pay you," I promised.

Alice stopped skipping. "How much?" she asked.

"A penny," I said. "It's all I've got."

"Not enough. Not enough for what I know!"

I groaned. Elsie Brown said, "I'll give you a penny as well. Two pennies ... please, Alice, please!"

"Bring the money to the churchyard gate this afternoon and I may tell you," she said.

I ran home and stole a penny from the money we got for selling some lambs at market. Dad would beat me if he ever found out. But it would be worth the beating.

Elsie and I handed over our pennies to Alice as we huddled in the gateway to the churchyard, trying to hide from the bitter wind that swept over the moors.

"So, did the Vampire kill her?" I asked.

Alice leaned forward. "It stepped through the open window and walked towards rotten Miss Ransome. She fell back onto the bed and it reached out its bony claws and gripped her by the shoulders. Then it leaned forward and ... and ... have you any more pennies for me?" she asked sweetly.

"No," I said angrily. "If you don't tell me, I'll just go and ask my dad what happened."

Alice blew out her cheeks. "Oh, very well. It leaned forward and bit her on the neck!"

"Urgh!" Elsie squealed and clutched her throat.

"Ahhhh!" Alice cried and slapped her hand against her throat. When she took her hand away it was dripping red.

"Alice! Has he got you?" I wailed.

She opened her eyes and looked at me. "Oh, Tommy, my dear Tommy ..." she croaked.

"Yes, Alice?"

"If I die ... then you don't get your penny back," she said.

"No, Alice," I moaned. "Don't die."

She gasped. "Oh, Tommy ... no one ever died from crushing a berry to her throat!" She opened her hand and showed me the red mush she had crushed at her throat. Then she smiled and wiped the hand against my cheek. "Fooled you ... again," she sighed. "Poor little Tommy."

Alice was cruel to me. Elsie told me it was Alice's way of showing that she likes me. Aren't girls strange?

"Did Miss Ransome die?" I asked.

"Ah, that's another story for another penny," Alice said.

I walked off to the fields to find my dad to ask him. "Oh, Tommy!" Alice called after me. "I'll tell you, Tommy."

Chapter 5
The Brother

"When the attacker bit her neck, Amelia found her voice and screamed," Alice said. "That seemed to scare him and he turned and ran back over the lawn to the graveyard. Edward Ransome heard the screams and grabbed a gun. But by the time he'd broken down Amelia's door, the man had escaped."

I looked back over the churchyard. The winter winds had made many old gravestones lean and tumble. Only one tomb stood strong.

It was like a small house. It had an iron gate and there were steps down to a stout oak door below the ground.

"Why escape into the churchyard?" Elsie asked.

"Maybe this is where the Vampire lives. This is where he'd escape," I said.

"None of the graves are dug up," Alice said.

"Vampires can sink through the earth and into their coffins," I said.

Alice gave a harsh laugh. "Don't be stupid, Tommy. You know nothing about vampires. If it can sink through earth, why couldn't it walk through her windows? It had to smash the glass."

"The only place he could go would be this tomb," I told her.

"That's the Perkins family tomb," Elsie said.

"How do you know?" Alice asked.

"Because my ma taught me how to read. And it says on the side – 'Here lie the Perkins family of Croglin. Parsons of this parish since 1660.'"

We heard the rattle of coach wheels on gravel and ran back to the wall to see. The black coach with white horses was standing in front of Croglin Hall.

The coachmen lifted a large wooden trunk that stood beside the Hall door. They loaded it onto the roof of the coach and fastened it with leather straps.

"Those will be all her fine clothes," Alice said.

The front door opened and Edward Ransome led his sister out. She was leaning on him. He was half carrying her and had to lift her into the coach. The poor angel had a scarf wrapped around her throat – the throat the Vampire had bitten. She looked pale as moonlight and ready to faint. Edward went back to the house, locked the door and climbed into the carriage with his sister.

"The other brother, Michael, is away in Penrith," Alice said.

"How do you know that?" I asked.

"I know a lot of things," she said with a smirk. "I know milky-faced Amelia is going to the seaside to recover. The brothers have rented Croglin Hall for seven years. They will stay here. But the weedy Amelia won't be back."

I was sad. It was as if an angel had landed in the village and now had flown away. I mean, Alice was lovely ... even without the tooth. But she wasn't like Amelia Ransome.

I hated the Vampire for driving her away. I wished I could catch him and destroy him.

Now Alice said Angel Amelia wouldn't be back. But clever Alice wasn't always right. And, this time, clever Alice was wrong.

Winter brought the snows and hunger and frost-bitten feet. The church was draughty and half empty now.

April was wet and the village lane was deep in mud.

Mud splashed the legs of the white horses as they trotted towards Croglin Hall pulling the black coach. The heavy wooden trunk was on the roof.

I ran through the churchyard to look over the wall.

The coach door opened and Amelia Ransome stepped down into the waiting arms of her brothers. “How are you?” they cried happily.

“Wonderful.” She laughed. “And this time I am here to stay.”

Suddenly winter was gone.

Chapter 6
The Vampire

The Angel Amelia and her brothers were welcome back in the village. Even the bad-tempered Michael went to the tavern and bought drinks for his workers on Croglin Hall Farm.

I was in the tavern tap room one evening, buying a jug of ale for my dad. Michael Ransome sat at a table with some cow herds. They smoked pipes that filled the room with a fog. Michael looked out of the window. "It's getting dark," he said and rose to his feet.

"Can't you stay a little longer, sir?" one of the men asked. He looked at his empty ale mug and was hoping to see it filled.

"No. We never leave Amelia alone in the Hall after dark," Michael Ransome said. "Not after ... last time."

"Last time," the men at the tables muttered.

"Edward and I sleep with loaded pistols by our beds. Another attack could kill Amelia. If that monster returns we'll be ready," he said and looked around the room. It was a warning. Michael went out into the summer night.

The men looked into their mugs. "A gun isn't much good against a vampire," one said.

"You can't kill a vampire with a bullet ... unless it's a silver bullet."

The men sucked on their pipes, silent, and I went home. Alice was playing in the lane with Elsie Brown.

They were playing with dolls made of straw, the way girls do. "Nice dolls," I said.

Alice stood up and waved one in my face. "No, Tommy, this one's a vampire and it's going to bite that one on the neck!" she said. Elsie Brown screamed as Alice turned her doll towards Elsie's.

"It's not a game," I said, angry. "Another attack could kill Amelia."

Alice looked sly. "It could be a game," she said. "We could have a game of Hunt the Vampire!"

"You mean ... you hide your vampire doll and we hunt for it?" I asked.

"No, stupid Tommy. We hunt the real Vampire. We hide in the churchyard and watch where it goes," she said.

"In the churchyard?" I gasped. "At night?"

"Scared?"

"No!" I said, too loud. "No. If nothing happens it would be so boring!"

Alice shrugged. "But if something does happen it will be the most exciting thing in your little life, little Tommy."

"We can't wait, night after night, for a vampire to appear," I said.

"Just one night," Elsie Brown blurted. "Alice says it will be tonight!"

I looked at Alice in the near-dark. "Tonight?"

"It's a full moon ... the same as last time. The Vampire walks when the moon is full," she murmured and her words made me shiver. "Scared? Little Tommy?"

"No."

I took my dad's ale into the house, grabbed a piece of bread and some cheese and hurried out. The moon was rising over the purple mountains as we slipped into the silent churchyard.

"We need to hide in the darkest corner," Alice said. "We don't want the Vampire to see us and suck our blood, do we, Elsie?"

"Nnnng!" Elsie said and shuddered.

The grass on the graves was soft and still warm from the summer sun. The moon crept across the sky. The church clock struck the hours. Ten, then 11, then 12.

On the last stroke of midnight we saw a shadow move across the churchyard. It seemed to come from the church door – or maybe from the great, grey Perkins tomb. It climbed over the low wall into the garden of Croglin Hall.

Elsie and Alice and I rose to our feet. We could see the window of Amelia Ransome's room, lit by a candle inside. The shadow shuffled across the lawn, towards the light, like a moth to the flame.

In the silence we heard the scritch-scratch of a claw against the glass. Inside the room we saw Amelia move into the candlelight and clutch at her throat. She looked as if she wanted to scream, but no sound came.

Scritch-scratch, then tap-tap-tap as the claw hammered at the glass. Crack! As the pane broke.

Still Amelia stood frozen and helpless. Suddenly a howl, like all the ghosts of Croglin churchyard, spilt the night air. “Aiiiieeee!”

It was Elsie Brown, screaming in terror. The monster at the window stopped and looked back towards us. It turned away from the window and began to cross the lawn.

Too late. Elsie’s scream had woken Michael Ransome. We saw him burst into Amelia’s room. Angel Amelia pointed a dumb finger at the window. The young man threw it open and looked across the lawn.

The monster was near the safety of the churchyard wall as Michael raised his pistol.

He fired. The monster screeched and jumped clear over the wall. It limped over the

churchyard as Michael Ransome sped over the garden. We ran to meet him. "Which way did it go?" he cried.

"Across the churchyard," I said stupidly.

"I know that, you fool, but where?"

I felt my face glow with shame. "I didn't see."

Alice looked down at the ground. "I didn't see," she mumbled.

The churchyard was empty now. "He didn't have time to reach the gate," Michael raged. "He must have gone into the church."

"Or the Perkins tomb," Alice said quietly.

The young man sighed. "It's too dark to search now. At first light we'll have the whole village search for him. I think I wounded him in the right leg," he said, looking at the empty pistol. “Next time I will destroy him – man or monster, I will send him back to the Hell he came from.”

Chapter 7
The Parson

Of course I didn't sleep.

At some time in the darkest hour I'll swear I heard pistol shot. It was muffled and far away. But it made me pull the blanket over my head and hide from the horrors of the night.

At dawn I got up and joined the villagers huddled at the church gate. Michael and Edward Ransome stood there, grim-faced in the early light. We were all ready to hunt for the Vampire.

The villagers were armed with anything they could find. Hay-forks and reaping hooks, knives and corn-flails. I took a wooden spoon from the kitchen.

Alice clutched at her straw doll. Her father carried a torch of twisted straw dipped in tar. It flickered and spat. “My Alice says we should look in the Perkins tomb,” he said. “We’ll need light.”

“The church or the tomb? Let’s look in the church first,” Edward Ransome said and led the way.

Candles burned on the altar and lit the pale face of Parson Perkins. He was sitting at the front of the church, all by himself. “You’re up early, Parson,” Michael Ransome said.

“Praying for you,” Parson Perkins said. He twisted his skinny hands together.

The stone floor of the church was clean. It had been newly scrubbed. "No trail of blood," Michael said to his brother. He looked to the parson. "May we search your family tomb?" he asked.

"It's locked," the parson said quickly.

"Then give me the key."

Parson Perkins reached to his belt and unhooked a bunch of keys. "Come and get it, sir," he said.

As the church clock chimed seven we were opening the door to the tomb. "The lock and the hinges are well greased," Alice's father said, as he led the way with the torch.

There were more steps down into a large room under the ground. The smell of rotting flesh would make even a strong stomach sick. As I pushed through the villagers along with

Alice, the sight we saw made us forget the smell.

There were a dozen coffins in there. Eleven had been broken open and the twisted funeral sheets and bones were scattered over the floor. Eyeless skulls stared up at us with teeth as rotten as Parson Perkins'.

The last coffin was open, but the corpse inside had not been disturbed. We looked down and the torch-light showed a hideous figure ... a corpse that was shrunken and dry like a mummy. Its face a brown mask with glowing eyes.

"That's the face we saw last night," Alice said quietly.

Michael Ransome crouched beside the coffin. "And look at the leg. That's a bullet hole in the left leg! I didn't believe in vampires," he said softly.

"You do now," a villager muttered.

"We must burn it," Michael Ransome said angrily. "Carry the coffin out, you men. We'll take it into the daylight – vampires can't stand daylight. It can't harm you out there. Let it burn on earth ... then let it burn in Hell."

The children ran into the woods to collect firewood and piled it into a huge bonfire in Croglin churchyard. I even threw in our wooden spoon. The mummy was placed on top. Mr Marley threw his torch onto the wood.

It crackled and smoked and then began to roar. The corpse curled up in the heat – almost as if it could feel the flames. The Vampire burned more fiercely than the wood. In an hour there were only smoking ashes left.

The villagers trooped into the church and Parson Perkins said prayers for the living.

"A great evil has been lifted from our village today," he said in his whining voice. "Go home safe and joyful!"

We left the church.

On Sundays Parson Perkins would stand at the church door and speak to everyone as they left. That morning he stood at the altar where we had seen him at dawn and he stayed there.

I turned for home.

I felt a tug at my sleeve. It was Alice. "Hide, Tom, hide!"

"What?" Her eyes were burning and excited. I thought the adventure had driven her mad.

She dragged me down the steps into the Perkins tomb. The oak door was locked again now.

"We can't go in there!" I cried.

"Hush! We're not. We're going to watch."

"Watch what?" I moaned, afraid and cold in the shadow of the stairway.

"Watch," she hissed.

We looked out over Croglin churchyard.

After a while the church door opened. Parson Perkins looked around, careful and sly. There was no one else in sight. He didn't see us half-hidden under the ground.

He began to walk towards his house. The house where he lived alone. "Too ugly to marry," Alice said softly. Then she said, "See?"

I saw.

Parson Perkins walked slowly, dragging his right leg. Limping ... as if he had been wounded.

Epilogue

The Vampire of Croglin Hall is said to be a true story. There were two attacks on a young woman who lived there with her brothers.

A family tomb was broken open, a shrunken corpse was found with damage to a leg and it was burned.

But was it a vampire ... a monster that sleeps by day and seeks human blood by night?

Or was it a mad human, who used the foolish fears of the villagers to terrify the poor people of Croglin?

I am not saying vampires exist. I am not saying vampires don't exist. This story is just one way to explain the old legend.

So? Are there really such things as vampires?

You decide.

Our books are tested
for children and young people by
children and young people.

Thanks to everyone who consulted on
a manuscript for their time and effort in
helping us to make our books better
for our readers.